KoKo Bear's New Potty

A Practical Parenting™
Read-Together Book

Vicki Lansky

Illustrated by Jane Prince

T0124909

Book Trade Distribution
Publishers Group West

Book Peddlers
Minnetonka, Mn

KOKO BEAR'S NEW POTTY
Bantam Books / 1986
Book Peddlers / 1997

Art Design and layout by MacLean & Tuminelly
Cover and interior art by Jane Prince

ISBN 0-916773-25-6

For group sales or quantity discounts contact:
Book Peddlers
15245 Minnetonka Boulevard
Minnetonka, MN 55345
612/912-0036

06 07 08   10 9

Printed in China by Pettit Network Inc

Introduction

Toilet training, I believe, is part of an overall urge towards independence and self-reliance that is natural for every child growing up. It is not something you do for children but rather something you help them learn for themselves.

One way you can help is by letting your child understand what to expect and what's expected. With that in mind, the story of KoKo Bear, a loveable little bear, will set an example for your child. KoKo Bear's transition from diapers to independent use of the toilet is a delightful story that you and your child will enjoy reading again and again.

To help you make this a smooth transition, there are tips and suggestions for parents and caregivers on every page. You can skim these silently while you and your child read about KoKo. For more detailed material and additional tips, you may wish to refer to my companion book, Practical Parenting *TOILET TRAINING*.

Every child is different, therefore readiness for toilet training will be slightly different for each child. Flexibility, gentleness and generous use of praise on your part can make this an easy and pleasant time for both of you.

Please remember, if you find yourself frustrated about your child's progress, that toilet training is a teaching and learning process, not an obedience issue nor a test that must be passed on any set date.

Sincerely,

Vicki Lansky

This is KoKo Bear. KoKo used to be a tiny little bear cub.

Now KoKo is growing up. Doing things for yourself is part of growing up.

What things can you do for yourself? Can you brush your teeth? Can you dress yourself?

- *Praise your child for independent behavior and attempts at self-help.*
- *Discuss with your child the things he or she can already do independently.*
- *Encourage your child's sense of self and control over his or her own world by allowing the extra time it takes to perform these tasks.*

KoKo wears diapers. When a diaper is dry, it feels comfy and cozy. KoKo likes the way a dry diaper feels.

Sometimes MaMa Bear asks, "KoKo, does your diaper still feel dry?"

KoKo thinks and says, "Yes, MaMa, it's dry."

- *Help your child learn to recognize and identify the sensations of dryness and wetness by using the terms "wet" and "dry" whenever you change a diaper.*
- *Talk about the pleasures of being clean and dry.*
- *Change diapers often to help him or her get used to and prefer the feel of a dry diaper.*

When a diaper gets full or wet, it doesn't feel comfy and cozy. KoKo doesn't like the way a messy diaper feels.

"PaPa," says KoKo, "I need a clean, dry diaper."

PaPa Bear says, "Why, KoKo, what a big bear you are to tell me. Come, let's put on a dry diaper now."

- *Wanting to please you is a good sign of your child's readiness for toilet training. Be pleased and praise your child for telling you about a wet or full diaper.*
- *Explain to your child why a diaper feels full or wet. It will help establish the cause-effect relationship.*
- *Talk about the sensation of "going" or being "about to go." Your child's recognition of these is another sign of readiness.*

KoKo knows that grown-up bears don't wear diapers. Grown-ups use the toilet in the bathroom.

Girls always sit down to use the toilet.

Boys sometimes sit down and sometimes stand up. That's because their bodies are different.

When MaMa Bear goes (*pee-pee**) or (*poo-poo**), she sits down on the toilet.

* *Substitute your familiar family words for urination and bowel movement when you see the parenthesis here and throughout the book.*
* *Decide early—before training begins—which family words to use. Then be consistent with your child. Avoid words like "yucky" that imply body functions or parts are dirty or disgusting.*
* *Let your child see you or others—a parent, an older sibling—use the toilet at home. Children learn by imitating.*

When PaPa Bear goes (*poo-poo*), he sits down on the toilet like MaMa Bear. But when he goes (*pee-pee*), he stands up in front of the toilet.

Sometimes growing-up boys don't stand in front of the toilet right away. They have to wait to get taller. So they sit down to go (*pee-pee*).

- *Going to the bathroom involves many separate acts—from removing pants to using toilet paper. Tell your child what you expect—don't assume he or she knows.*
- *Discuss your timing and approach to toilet training with your spouse and any other caregivers. All adults close to the child should be consistent.*
- *While bowel control usually proceeds bladder control, this is not always the case. Often for boys, in particular, this pattern is reversed.*

One day PaPa Bear brings home something special.

"Look, KoKo," he says. "Here is a potty chair for you. You can use it whenever you have to go (*pee-pee* or *poo-poo*). That way your diaper can stay clean and dry."

"This is just the right size for me," thinks KoKo.

- *Let your child "practice" sitting on the potty chair with or without clothes. This will help a child feel familiar and comfortable with this new addition.*
- *Be sure your child's clothing is easy to pull on and off. Avoid buttons, snaps and belts during this period.*
- *You don't have to have a potty chair for training. Especially for children trained later, this intermediate aid may not be needed.*

KoKo tries sitting on the potty chair without a diaper. It is fun to sit there like a grown-up. But nothing happens! The (*pee-pee* or *poo-poo*) doesn't come!

"That's okay, KoKo," says MaMa. "That was a good try. The time just wasn't right for you. We'll try again later."

- *Praise your child whenever he or she is willing to sit and try to go. For some children, sitting for longer than 10 seconds is progress! And don't expect a "performance" every time.*
- *In the beginning, be prepared to keep your child company in the bathroom. To help the time pass, try reading a story aloud.*
- *You may need to prompt your child with an occasional "It's time to try now." If you get a "no!" don't push it. Respect your child's limits.*

Later KoKo says, "MaMa, I have to go."

MaMa says, "Good, KoKo, let's go sit on your potty chair." Sure enough, this time KoKo goes (*pee-pee*).

"Oh, KoKo, I'm SO proud of you," says MaMa Bear. She gives KoKo a big warm bear hug.

KoKo is proud and happy too.

- *Praise your child for every deposit he or she makes in the potty chair or toilet during this early learning stage.*
- *Don't expect your child to do everything in the potty chair or toilet from the first day on. It is a variable process of stops and starts.*
- *Look for a regular pattern or indicator suggesting he or she is about "to go." If there is none, then thirty minutes after a meal is usually a good time to try.*

KoKo now has clean, dry diapers most of the time. One day MaMa surprises her little bear with a present.

"Look, KoKo," she says. "Here are some Big-Bear pants just for you."

KoKo loves the Big-Bear pants and puts them on right away. KoKo will try to keep them clean and dry.

- *Try whatever rewards or incentives seem appropriate to you—material or nonmaterial. The use of rewards is a viable part of the training process for many parents and does not last forever.*
- *When you buy "grown-up" or training pants, be sure they are loose enough around the legs for your child to raise and lower them easily.*
- *For some children, the trip to the store to help pick out pants adds to the excitement and motivation for successful use of the potty chair or toilet.*

Every time KoKo goes to the potty, MaMa Bear empties the pot into the toilet. Then she rinses it out in the sink. She lets KoKo flush the toilet.

"Whoosh," says KoKo.

"Now it's time to wash your paws," MaMa says.

Can you flush the toilet? Do you wash your hands by yourself?

- *It's up to you to decide whether you want your child to empty his or her own potty chair. Some parents feel that this should be the child's responsibility; some don't.*
- *Be sensitive to your child's fears about flushing. Some children find the noise frightening. Others wonder why their parents don't want to keep the "prize" they've just left!*
- *Keep a sturdy child's bench or step-stool in the bathroom to make it easier for your child to reach the sink.*

Soon KoKo is big enough to use the toilet, just like PaPa and MaMa Bear. KoKo's own special seat fits right on top of the toilet.

KoKo uses the toilet every day.

"Good going, KoKo," says MaMa Bear.

"Nice work, KoKo," says PaPa Bear. "We are very proud of you."

- *Remember that the toilet can seem awfully big to your child. An adapter seat and a step-stool can make the toilet seat feel more secure.*
- *If you don't have an adapter seat, let your child sit on the toilet facing sideways or even backwards for a more secure position.*
- *Keep toilet paper on the back of the toilet if the holder isn't within easy reach of your child's shorter arms.*

One day KoKo doesn't get to the bathroom soon enough. KoKo's pants get wet. The floor gets wet. KoKo gets wet. Ish! KoKo feels sad.

MaMa Bear helps KoKo clean up and put on dry clothes.

"It's okay, KoKo," she says. "Everybody has accidents sometimes." Then she gives KoKo a hug and kiss. "You are a good bear and I love you."

KoKo's sad feelings go away.

- *Frequent accidents may be caused by allergies, illnesses or other physical conditions. Consider having your child checked by a doctor.*
- *Never punish your child for an accident. Clean up in a matter-of-fact way. A child who is anxious to please may agonize over what is perceived as shameful behavior.*
- *Separate feelings of disappointment over an accident from disapproval of your child. Avoid phrases like "bad boy"—"bad girl."*

KoKo still wears diapers to bed. KoKo hasn't learned to stay dry all night.

"When can I wear my pants to bed?" KoKo asks.

"When you get older. It will be easier to stay dry at night then," MaMa says. "Don't worry."

"For now, KoKo, you're as grown-up as you can be," PaPa says. "And we think you're the best growing-up bear in the whole wide world!"

- *Night-time control requires children to master involuntary muscles while they sleep. For some children it can take months or even years after they've learned daytime control.*
- *You can try limiting fluid intake after dinner and waking your child for a trip to the bathroom before you go to bed, but there is no guarantee that these techniques will be successful.*
- *Praise your child whenever he or she makes it through the night with dry diapers.*

KoKo knows there are toilets in many places away from home. KoKo likes to visit the bathrooms in restaurants. Do you like that too?

MaMa or PaPa Bear takes KoKo to the bathroom.

Each door has a picture. There is one for boys and one for girls. Which door should KoKo open?

- *Always accompany your child to public restrooms. Most mothers feel comfortable taking little boys into ladies' room; for fathers with little girls this can be more difficult. Use your judgment.*
- *Some children are afraid to use strange bathrooms. Respect their fears. This stage passes quickly, as most stages do.*
- *Remember that there are three things you cannot do for your child: **eat—sleep—or go to the bathroom!***

Other Parenting Books by Vicki Lansky

- Feed Me! I'm Yours
  - The Taming Of The CANDY Monster
    - Games Babies Play
      - Practical Parenting Tips Yrs.1–5
        - Toilet Training
          - KoKo Bear's New Potty
            - Birthday Parties
              - Welcoming Your Second Baby
                - A New Baby At KoKo Bear's House
                  - KoKo Bear's Big Earache
                    - Getting Your Child to Sleep... And Back to Sleep
                      - Trouble-Free Travel With Children

- Baby Proofing Basics • Dear Babysitter Handbook • Divorce Book For Parents • 101 Ways To Tell Your Child *I Love You* • 101 Ways To Make Your Child Feel Special •101 Ways To Be A Special Dad • 101 Ways To Be A Special Mom • 101 Ways To Spoil Your Grandchild • Kids Cooking • Microwave Cooking For Kids

For a free catalog of all books by Vicki Lansky
or to place a credit card order, write to
Practical Parenting
Dept KNP, Minnetonka, MN 55345-1510
or call 1-800-255-3379

Folding Potty Seat Adapter
Convenient plastic folds to a 5+"
square. Fits standard toilet seats.
$12.95 plus $4.00 s/h